MATCHBOX AND THE CHEEKY SHEEP

Written by Carole York and
illustrated by Carol Murray

DEDICATION

This book is dedicated to
all the abused horses and
ponies in Ireland.
Abandoned by both their
owners and their government

CHAPTER ONE-MATCHBOX COMES

TO STAY

I am a little coloured
Shetland pony and I'm seven
years old. My name is
Matchbox but at first the
lady called me by alot of
other names because I used
to be a very naughty pony.

It wasn't my fault I was so badly behaved, I had a miserable life before I came here.

I was dumped in the woods and then I was rescued and sent to a home with two other Shetlands and a small donkey called Twinkle but it wasn't a nice place. The man beat me about the head alot, and the donkey too. When word got out that we were being cruelly treated the rescue people came to take us all back but it was too late for the other two Shetlands. They had disappeared.

The nasty man said they'd been stolen but I knew the truth because I'd seen him selling them off to another man.

He wanted to sell me off too but I bit the man so he wouldn't take me, that was the only time being a kicker and a biter turned out to be a good thing because they never found those other two ponies, nobody knows what happened to them.

The rescue people came early one morning. Their names were Ann and Pete. We saw them letting down the ramp and they were arguing with the nasty man so I said to Twinkle, come on here's our chance, let's get on the box while they're not looking, so we ran out and barged past Ann and ran into the box.

I felt sorry for the other two ponies who'd been sold but it was my lucky day because otherwise there would have been no room in the box for me.

The little donkey got a good home very quickly but nobody wanted me on account of my bad manners.

I was sent out a few times to different places because I'm a very pretty little pony but looks aren't everything and when people realised I had a mean streak they sent me back to the rescue.

A little while later a lady called Georgia took me in.

It went well at first but then I started fighting with her ponies so I couldn't stay there either. Luckily for me, Georgia knew this lady and asked her to take me. At first the lady said no, she already had too many ponies but then she changed her mind and I came down here in a box with another pony called Snip. He was very big. We had to travel all the way from Kildare and I was very nervous.
Snip was a friendly pony and he told me not to be frightened.

The Lady had taken his friend Dotty the year before and she'd written him a letter to say how nice it was.

He was twelve years old and he told me him and Dotty had been together since he was a foal and he was very sad when they took her away. He couldn't wait to see her again.

"It might be our forever home," he said, but I didn't think it would be my forever home because I was always sent back to the rescue.

When we got off the box I
saw other ponies in the
fields and they all called
to us, asking us what were
our names and where were we
from and Snip said we were
from up the country.

The lady put Snip and me
into a small paddock on our
own because ponies can be
funny about new ponies and
sometimes they chase you
all over and bite you when
they catch you so it's
better if you're on your
own and can introduce
yourself over the fence.

And then Snip's friend
Dotty came running down the
track and the lady let her
in with us and after that
Snip took no notice of me
any more he was so happy to
see his friend.
I felt sad. I don't make
friends easily, because I
like to fight with
everyone.
Soon a small palomino came
to look at me, she said her
name was Pamela Anderson
and she was the lead mare
and I was never to call her
Pam or Pamela, unless I
wanted my ears boxed.

She said I was always to
call her by her full name
but I didn't think I was
going to take orders from
her, lead mare or no lead
mare and I told her so and
she said I had an attitude
problem and walked away.
Then a chestnut Welsh pony
came, he said his name was
Diablo. He wasn't very
nice.
"Oy. You. We don't like
ponies with blue eyes," he
said. "It's unnatural."
I told him I couldn't help
it that I had one blue eye,
it's the way I was born and
nothing I can do about it.

I'd had the same problem in the places I was in before. Nobody seems to like a pony with a blue eye. They said it made them nervous because they couldn't figure out what I was going to do next.

Then a little black pony came shuffling down the track looking very excited but when she got closer she stared at me and looked sad.

"Oh. I thought you were Freddie," she said.

"He was my friend when I
lived with the nasty
people. You look just like
him essept for that tear in
your nostril. How did you
get that?"
"They tied me to a fence
and I caught it on the
barbed wire," I replied.
She said she was a Ninja
Shetland. I'd never heard
of a Ninja Shetland before.
She had shoulders that
stuck out and she walked
funny.
She said she was born like
that and in the cold
weather her shoulders hurt
her but the lady was trying
to fix her.

She was only eighteen
months old and she'd been
thrown out on the road when
she was a foal.
"Don't mind that Diablo,
he's a fiend, but he's
mostly all talk. If you
stay out of his way he
won't bother you," she
said.
I thought, I'm not going to
stay out of anybody's way,
I'm not afraid of anyone,
but I kept it to myself
because she was a nice pony
and she was only trying to
help me. She said she was
the lady's favourite pony.

I thought it must be nice to be someone's favourite pony. I'd never been anyone's favourite pony. There were three other black Shetland ponies, a boy and and two girls. The boy pony's name was Super Mario and he had sore feet because when they found him his feet turned up like slippers because he hadn't seen a farrier for ten years. The lady spent hours every week trimming his feet until she cut her hand and had to go to hospital for six stitches. After that she got the farrier in.

The girl ponies were called
Frances and Diamond. Diamond
was seven years old and she
was the fattest pony I'd
ever seen.

After two days of chit chat
across the fence the lady
let me out of the paddock
onto the track and Diablo
came up to me right away,
all puffed up and cocky.
"Let's fight," he said.
I stared at him for a
minute.
"You don't want to fight
me. I'm a good fighter," I
replied.

"What? You're only an itty bitty thing," he said and he laughed.

That made me cross, I don't like being laughed at, so I jumped up and smacked him with my front feet.

We had a right old go, in the middle of the track, kicking and biting and everybody watching.

Pamela Anderson said we were at it for half an hour, she being the timekeeper and referee.

Nobody won the fight so we declared a truce and said we'd take it up another day.

CHAPTER TWO-MATCHBOX RUNS AWAY

I'd been there a week when
I did a bad thing. I bit
the lady.
I didn't mean to do it.

I knew it was wrong but she got me in a corner and put out her hand too quickly and I thought she was going to hit me.

Pamela Anderson was very,very cross.

"How could you bite the lady?" she said. " She was only trying to put dip on you to stop you getting lice."

I said I didn't have any lice and I didn't like the smell of the dip but Pamela Anderson said she didn't care, I had no business biting the lady and nobody wanted to talk to me after that.

I was sure I was going to
be sent back to the rescue
then, so after two weeks
and still nobody talking to
me I ran away and hid in
next door's field.
The lady came twice a day
with a bucket of feed to
try and get me back, but
I'd never seen feed before
and I didn't know what it
was.
So I said, you can leave
that over there by the
ditch and I'll have a look
at it later.
I felt very lonely. I
pretended I didnt care but
I did.

Then it started to rain and soon the corner where I'd got out became a big lake. It came over the lady's wellies and she couldn't bring the feed any more. She went and stood on top of the hill at the bottom of our field where she could see me and shouted at me.

"Matchbox! I'm warning you. If you don't get your fat pony bottom back over this ditch right now there's going to be trouble!"
"What kind of trouble?" I replied.

That made her really cross
and she called me a little
basket. I don't know why
she got so exercised, I was
only trying to find out
whether it was worth coming
back or not.

She said she was going to
wait until the rain stopped
and the lake got shallower
and then she was coming to
get me and then I'd find
out what kind of trouble.

Waiting for rain to stop in
Ireland is a bit like
waiting for the goviment to
do something about all the
ponies that get beaten and
starved and thrown out onto
the roads.

I didn't think she'd be coming to get me any time soon.

It was another three weeks before the lady could walk through the lake and she came with a bucket of feed and Pamela Anderson.

Pamela Anderson takes care of all the new ponies when they first arrive. She's training to be a therapy pony for ponies.

She was supposed to persuade me to come home but when she saw all the grass in the field she ran away from the lady and wouldn't come back.

So now there were two of us
in there. We galloped
around that field, the lady
running behind us calling
us all sorts of names, it
was the best craic ever.
Pamela Anderson said we'd
best enjoy it while we
could because it wouldn't
last long, we'd made the
lady so mad we were
probably going to end up in
jail for six weeks.
She was right.

The Lady came back the next
day with Paddy O'Donnell
and Orla and they hunted us
back over that ditch so
fast I thought my legs
would fall off.

And the Lady put us in the
high security paddock for
naughty ponies where
Frances used to live until
she started behaving
herself.
The high security paddock
has four strands of wire
around it and it runs off
its own battery fencer.

I was never going to behave myself so I thought I'd be in there forever but I didn't mind too much because there were loads of places to hide. I found a place up against the ditch, behind a tree where nobody could see me and waited to see if anyone would come to make friends with me but nobody did. Pamela Anderson said if I stopped fighting with everyone I might make some friends but I didnt think there was any point because I was bound to be sent back to the rescue sooner or later.

And then I saw the
strangest thing. A one eyed
mouse came up to me riding
a black and white cat. He
said his name was Gordon
and the cat was his pet.
The cat was blind in both
eyes. I'd seen alot of
things in all the places
I'd been but I'd never seen
a one eyed mouse who had a
blind cat for a pet.
The mouse said he'd be my
friend but he didn't have
time to stay and chat
because he was training the
cat for a Three Day Event
and he had to get on with
it.

When I asked him what a
Three Day Event was he said
it was a competition where
you have to dance and run
across the countryside and
jump over poles.

"You're training a blind
cat to dance and run and
jump?" I said.
"Yep."
"And how's that going for
you?"
"Not very well," the mouse
replied," that's why I've
no time to stop and chat."

Then he gave the cat a smack with a stick he was carrying. The cat took off and ran up the nearest tree and I didn't see either of them for quite some time after that.

The Little Ninja Shetland started coming into our field. She was so tiny she could get under the fence without getting a shock and she was in and out all the time. She said she'd be my friend so now I had two friends although I wasn't sure whether Gordon counted because he was a mouse.

It was the Ninja Shetland who taught me how to read and write so that I could keep on writing the books after she was gone. I didn't know what she meant by that but in the middle of summer I found out, when a very bad thing happened.

One night the Little Ninja Shetland lay down to rest and the next morning she couldn't get up. The Lady hadn't been able to fix her sticky out shoulders after all.

The vet came in the afternoon and made her go to sleep and we didn't see the lady for three days after, she never came out of the house once.

As for me, I didn't know how I'd manage without my friend. I was very sad and I thought I might run away and never come back.

"What are we going to do if she never comes out of the house again?" said Mario. I could see he was very worried by the way he scrunched up his eyes.

"She will," replied Pamela Anderson. "People are like that. They get very sad when anyone dies."

She called a meeting of the Pony Council and told us what we were going to do when the lady came out again.

Frances said she didn't think she could do it but Pamela Anderson told her to get over herself.

"You'll do it for the lady. Where would you be without her? Dead is where you'd be."

"I don't think I can do it either. I can't let people touch my head, I'll have a panic attack," I said.

"You be having more than a panic attack if you don't do as I say," replied Pamela Anderson. "I'll have you sent to the pound." Pamela Anderson could be very harsh sometimes. She was always threatening us with the pound and even thought the lady said she couldn't do it we were never quite sure.

So we did as she said most of the time just in case. When the lady came out after the three days she went to sit under the big tree on the track, it was her favourite place, she had an armchair there and all. We could see she was crying.

"Who's goin first?" said Diablo.

"Who do you think's goin first? Me, of course. Now get in line like I told you to," replied Pamela Anderson.

We all lined up behind
Pamela Anderson but Frances
couldn't remember where she
was supposed to go.
Frances can't remember
anything from one day to
the next because she got
brain damage from being
abused for her whole life.
We put her in the middle so
she couldn't get away, and
me behind her, and Diablo
and Snip and Dotty behind
me.
Mario was at the back
because he was so slow we'd
have been at it a week if
we'd let him go in front.

Then we walked up to the
Lady and when we got there
we offered her our heads to
touch. It wasn't so bad and
I thought I might let the
Lady do it again one day.
When Frances did it the
Lady cried even more, I
don't know why.

After the little Ninja
Shetland died Frances
became the Lady's favourite
and went to be the garden
pony.

Everybody except Pamela
Anderson wanted to be the
garden pony because you got
special privileges like
treats if you waited long
enough outside the back
door and in winter you got
fed first.

Pamela Anderson said she
didn't need to be anyone's
favourite because she was
so beautiful that everyone
loved her and gave her
treats the minute they saw
her.

Frances was supposed to keep the lawn tidy but she went into the veggie patch and pulled out all the carrots and and threw them aside, she didnt even eat them.

"She's gonna get a clattering now," said Diablo, but she didn't. The Lady just had a word with her and gave her more carrots out of the frijerator. Frances got away with murder.That was when I decided I wanted to be the Lady's favourite pony.

CHAPTER THREE- MACDONALD COMES TO STAY

I knew that getting to be the favourite pony wasn't going to be easy. I'd have to stop fighting and find ways to be helpful to the Lady.

I made a few mistakes along the way.

Once I heard her say she
had to move the fence posts
and it was going to take
her forever so I decided to
knock ten of them down to
help her but she said it
wasn't helpful at all and
locked me in the stable for
a whole day.
There was another time when
the lady said she was going
to kill Dog if she didn't
stop barking at us so I
kicked her in the throat.
It stopped her barking
alright but the lady was
very cross.

And there was the time I heard the lady say she was sick to death of us and I rang for the ambulance to bring her to hospital. That didn't go down well at all and Frances said I was stupid, the lady wasn't really sick, it was only a fibber of peas, which is what grown ups say when they want to confuse you. But I did stop fighting and Pamela Anderson gave me a bronze star when she went to give her weekly Pony Behaviour Report to the Lady.

Then one Sunday afternoon
we heard Mario roaring. He
was the watchpony and it
was his job to let the lady
know whenever someone
opened the gate.
When we looked up a box was
rattling down the driveway
and when they lowered the
ramp a tiny cob foal got
out.

He was white with black
patches on him and he was
screaming his head off. He
was only a week old, and he
cried for three days. The
lady called him MacDonald.

"Where's his mammy?" said Mario.

"She's gone off to take care of another foal that's going to be a racehorse," replied Pamela Anderson.

I didn't understand why they'd done that, when Macdonald was so young and when I asked Pamela Anderson she said they do it all the time but they keep it a secret.

The racehorse foal was more valuable than Macdonald so it couldn't be let die just because its own mammy had died.

I don't know how she knew
that but she always seemed
to know everything.
"But what about MacDonald?
Won't he die without his
mammy?"
"No he won't because the
Lady is going to be his
mammy now."
At first MacDonald was kept
in the stable and we
weren't allowed to touch
him.
The Lady had to feed him a
bucket of milk every four
hours, day and night,
because he couldn't eat by
himself.

We felt sorry for her, carrying the bucket down the track in the middle of the night, just as well it wasn't the middle of winter.

After three days MacDonald was let out into a small paddock on his own and he ran around all over and the lady had to put a headcollar and lunge rein on him to stop him running into the electric fence. He wasn't very bright.

It was when she let him out onto the track that the trouble began. He started with Pamela Anderson.

"Are you my mammy?" he
said.
"Nope."
Then he went to Frances and
asked her and she chased
him away and got punished
by the Lady for cursing.
He went to Diablo then.
"Are you my mammy?"
"Arragh, go away from me,
can't you see I'm a boy?"
Like I said, MacDonald
wasn't very bright.
He tried everyone and we
all said no we're not your
mammy and we thought that
was the end of it but he
came back the next day and
the day after that, he
wouldnt give up.

He was at it for a week and
then he went to the Lady
and asked her and she said
yes she was his mammy, just
to shut him up but soon she
was sorry she'd said it
because he started
following her around all
over and cried whenever she
went inside the house and
after a few weeks he
started jumping on her back
and biting her.
She said she wasn't having
that so she put him in a
paddock with me and told me
to put manners on him.

I was very proud to have
been given that job because
you only get a job if you
are well behaved, that's
why Diablo never got a job.
The lady said he was
possessed by the devil.
I knew this was my chance
to be the lady's favourite
pony so I took it very
seriously.
As soon as MacDonald came
in I ran at him and he got
such a fright he jumped
right out of the paddock.
We had a little talk over
the fence and I said he
could come back if he
behaved himself.

It was then that I saw he had one blue eye too and I thought, yay, he can be my friend because the others won't like him either. MacDonald was a very nice little foal and very respectful once I'd explained the rules to him, like don't jump on me and don't bite my bottom and don't kick me and don't hit me with your front hooves. Nobody likes a pony that bites and kick, just ask me.

CHAPTER FOUR-DIABLO GETS ARRESTED

The lady said she was very
pleased with my work and I
waited to see if she would
make me the favourite pony
but she didn't. I was
disappointed but I wasn't
going to give up and soon I
got another chance to be
helpful.

The sheep arrived on a
Thursday.
They were cull ewes and the
lady got them off a farmer
who didn't want them any
more because they were too
old to have lambs, which
was a good thing because we
didnt want to wake up one
morning and find there were
four of them. Or six, even,
if they had twins. They had
white coats and black faces
and the lady called them
Florence and Jemima. The
lady got them to eat the
ragwort because ragwort is
poisonous to ponies but not
to sheep. They love it.

The trouble was they didnt
do the job they were
employed to do and they
wouldn't stay where they
were supposed to be.
Soon everyone was grumbling
about those sheep.
Diablo went to see what
they were up to and when he
came back he was as mad as
a boxful of frogs.

"You hear them cheeky sheep? They not eating the ragwort. They eating our grass. I seen em munching it with their little pointy teeth and when I asked em why they weren't eating the ragwort they told me to mind my own business. They not even here a wet week, who do they think they are?"

"Yeah, look at them, they making all those tiny little poos everywhere, I'm spitting them out of my mouth the livelong day. Burst them out of it," said Frances.

One day I heard the Lady
telling the sheep she was
going to get rid of them if
they didn't start
behaving.Every pony gets a
chance to make a wish come
true once a year, nobody
can deny him, it's in the
Pony Rule Book. I decided
to give my wish to the Lady
but when I told Pamela
Anderson she said no, you
can't use your wish to
bring harm on other
animals.
"I'm not trying to harm
them, I'm just trying to
help the Lady," I said.

"The lady doesn't really want to get rid of them. She's only messing. She gave them names didn't she? Everyone knows if you give an animal a name you'll never get rid of it."

So that was the end of that idea.

Until Pamela Anderson got a mouthful of sheep poo and said that's it, those sheep have got to go.

First Diablo went to ask them nicely.

"I believe the grass is lovely in Wales. You'd like it there. And it's not far to swim," he said. "Look, you can see it from here."
"That's not Wales, you plonker, it's Brownstown Head but anyway there's no way we're swimming to Wales. We like it here."
"Grass is better in Wales," said Diablo
"And how would you know that? You were never out of Newry before you came here."
"It's in my genetic memory."
"Your what?"

"It's in my cells, like, from being a Welsh pony."

"Whats he on about?" said Jemima.

"Who knows? He's cracked. Anyway, we not leaving," said Florence.

Diablo came back and told us what the sheep had said. I could see it wasn't going to be easy to get rid of them.

Then the lady went away to West Cork for the weekend and Diablo said let's hunt those sheep down to Roisin's, she's loads of sheep, she'll never notice an extra two.

I wanted to go with them
but Pamela Anderson said I
was to stay behind and mind
MacDonald who couldn't be
left alone or he'd get up
to mischief.

"I'll help you. I'm a
trained sheepdog," said Dog
but she was the worst
sheepdog we'd ever seen.
She hadn't a clue.

She hunted them over the
ditch and into the road and
Diablo and Pamela Anderson
went to help her and they
were almost at Roisin's
when someone driving past
rang the guards and then
the sheep disappeared and
the guards wouldnt believe
Diablo.

"Where's the sheep then?
The ones you're driving to
Roisin's?" said the guard.
He was a very big guard and
he was very cross because
he'd been on his break when
he got called out.

"They were here a minute ago, guard, I dont know where they've gone," Diablo replied

"A likely story. Do you think I came down in the last rain shower?" said the guard.

Diablo said yes which is not something you say to a guard, even I know that and the guard went very red in the face and arrested them both and put them into Roisin's field and rang the Lady and she had to drive back from West Cork and ring Amanda to bring them home.

Diablo said he wasn't getting in the box so Pamela Anderson said if he wasnt getting in it neither was she.

The Lady had to chase them all over Roisin's field and it was half an hour before they got on the box and Amanda took them to hers. And while all that was going on half the parish was out looking for the sheep, Florence was nearly at the Metalman before they caught up with her, and they found Jemima down at Supervalu.

Dog told the Lady the sheep
had got out on their own
and she was only trying to
bring them back, her being
a trained sheepdog an all.

"Trained sheepdog? Dont
talk nonsense. You were
found wandering on the Cork
Road stinking and full of
fleas when you were twelve
weeks old."

Dog was cross about that, she didn't want us to know she was a stray.

"I taught myself off YouTube. Well, actually it was a cattle herding course I went on, like in Australia where the dogs jump on the cattle's backs. How was I to know them stupid sheep would lose their minds when I jumped on them?" she replied.

Dog was locked inside for a week and jumped on all the furniture in the sitting room and made things worse for herself.

The lady told me I was a
very good boy for staying
behind and minding
MacDonald while everyone
else was out causing
trouble and she gave me
extra carrots for a week
and Iwrote it in my little
notebook where I kept score
of all the times I'd helped
the lady so thatI'd know
when I was getting close to
becoming the favourite
pony.
Diablo and Pamela Anderson
were at Amanda's for weeks.
While they were away
MacDonald came up with an
idea.

"Let's ask the fairies to cast a spell on the sheep and make them walk off the cliffs into the sea at Kilfarrassey and swim to Wales," he said.

"What fairies?" said Frances.

"The fairies that live in the ditch."

"I never seen a fairy in the ditch."

"That's because only foals can see the fairies."

"Can't listen to him any more," said Mario. "Where does he get these notions? Someone shut him up."

"Fermented apples," replied Snip. "I seen him eating them in the orchard."

"Not," said MacDonald. "I really can see fairies. If you don't believe me come with me and I'll show you."

Frances said she'd go with him and when she came back she said, yes, she'd seen the fairies, there were two of them and six little baby fairies.

"What they look like?" asked Mario.

"Like rabbits."

Snip started laughing.

"If they look like rabbits then they most likely are rabbits," he said.

You couldn't trust anything Frances said because of the brain damage from all the abuse and as well as that she told alot of lies.

I don't know how she got to be the lady's favourite because she was a very grumpy pony and told so many lies.

We weren't sure whether to
believe her or not but in
the end it didn't matter
because the fairies or
rabbits or whatever they
were said they wouldn't
take part in it, the sheep
must have got to them
before us and paid them
off.

CHAPTER FIVE-THE FARRIER COMES

Word got out that the farrier was coming on Friday so Pamela Anderson called a Pony Council because the farrier is an emergency and you have to volunteer, same as when the dentist comes.

It's difficult getting ponies to volunteer for the farrier because we don't like our legs being touched. We wake up every morning wondering if we're going to be someone's breakfast and our legs are the only things that can get us away so we don't like people messing with them. Especially the farrier. What if a lion jumps out of the bushes whilst the farrier's holding up one of our legs? How are we going to run away on three legs?The lady told us there were no lions in Ireland but we didn't believe her.

"How does she know? Just
because she hasn't seen one
doesn't mean there aren't
any," said Pamela Anderson.
The Lady said she was a
drama queen and to stop
winding us up or she'd send
her back to Amanda's.
The way it works is the
Lady tells Pamela Anderson
how many ponies the
farrier's going to get,
it's usually only two at a
time unless the Lady got a
donation or got loads of
showjumpers to massage in
Kilkenny because they pay
her for that. The Lady
works very hard to keep us.

Then it might be three or
even four. After that
Pamela Anderson pulls the
name out of a hat. It's
like the Lotto only you
don't want the prize when
you win it.
My name wasn't put in the
hat because the last time
the farrier came I stood up
and whacked him in the
chest with both my front
feet and he said the lady
could make me into
sausages, he wasn't going
to trim my feet ever. That
hadn't helped my chances
either but I hoped I'd done
enough good things since to
make up for it.

That day it was Pamela
Anderson and Frances.
"What?" said Frances."You
must have made a mistake.
The lady never lets the
farrier near me cos I too
traumatised."
Frances used that long word
all the time to get out of
everything.
"Well she says it's time.
You been here three years
now."
"I don't care.I not lettin
no farrier near me."
"You have to. Your name
came up. It's the rules,"
said Pamela Anderson.

Friday came and went and
Frances locked up all day
in the shed waiting but the
farrier never came,
farriers are like that,
they never come when
they're supposed to, it's
to catch you off your
guard. Instead he came on
Tuesday.

When he picked up Frances's
front foot she knelt down
like a camel and when he
picked up her hind foot she
sat down like a dog.

She threw shapes around the stable, the farrier hanging onto her leg and the lady hanging onto her headcollar and then she lay down and refused to get up so the farrier had to kneel down beside her. He said some of the words the lady doesn't allow us to use.

The lady was mortified, she said let's leave it but the farrier said, I'm not letting a thirty four inch pony get the better of me so in the end she got her feet trimmed, all four of them.

When he was done with her
she shot out of that stable
like a rocket.
After that I thought
Frances might get a
demotion but she didnt. The
lady was very pleased with
her and gave her extra
carrots. I couldn't
understand why I got into
trouble for smacking the
farrier in the chest but
Frances got carrots for
dragging him all over the
stable and knocking the
lady to the ground.

We saw it all because
Pamela Anderson sold
tickets for a fiver each,
she said she outbid Sky and
the BBC for the exclusive
rights. I think that last
bit was a lie.
Afterwards Frances tried to
make out she'd put manners
on the farrier.
"I sorted him out," she
said. "He won't mess with
me again."
"Yeah right," said Diablo.

Anyway she got very cocky after that, prancing around in her new feet, all pared and tidy until Mario gave her a smack.

By then the Lady had given me a very important job on account of the improvement in my behaviour.

My job was to round up all the ponies for roll call and inspection every morning. I was sure it was only a matter of time before I replaced Frances as the favourite.

Everybody came when they were called and stood in a row in the top paddock under the big fir tree beside Rocketts and said if they had hurt themselves in the night or if they had sore tummies or sore feet and then I went to tell the Lady.

I only made one mistake on the day Mario disappeared and I lied to the Lady because I was too afraid to tell her I couldn't find him even after I'd looked all over.

The lady knew straight away
I was lying because she'd
sent him to Amanda's the
day before and forgotten to
tell me. I didnt get into
alot of trouble because the
lady understood why I'd
lied but she told me it's
always best to tell the
truth even if it gets you
into trouble.
She also said not
everything's your fault,
Matchbox.

And then Florence told MacDonald she was his mammy. He was only six months old and he believed her. She told him she'd run away from the foster farm to be with him. A story of such hardship and MacDonald believed every word of it and cried for days. He kept asking her to tell the story again and every time she told him it got worse and he cried even more.
I thought he was a dope but Pamela Anderson said it wasn't his fault.

If your real mammy goes missing when you're a baby you'll spend the rest of your life trying to make everyone your mammy. She said even if your mammy was there but she took no notice of you, you'd be the same. She said she'd learned that when she went on her course to become a Therapy Pony for Ponies. Pamela Anderson was a very clever pony.
MacDonald started going with Florence wherever she went and told us he was a sheep. He even started talking like a sheep. Baa baa baa, all day long.

It wasn't long before we were sick of him and Pamela Anderson called an emergency meeting of the Pony Council to tell him that he wasn't a sheep, and he was to stay away from Florence.

"But she's my mammy," he said.

"She is not. She's lying," replied Pamela Anderson.

"I don't believe you. Why would she do that?"

"Because she's a sheep and all sheep are liars."

I hadn't known that sheep are liars but I made a note to remember it in case I ever met any other sheep. By then my notebook was full of things I'd done for the lady and I was sure I would soon be her favourite pony.

"Do you look like Florence?" said Diablo.

MacDonald shook his head.

"Do you smell like her?" said Frances.

He shook his head again.

"Well then you're not a sheep are you?"

MacDonald looked at
Florence for a long time
and then he started
crying.He cried all night
and all of the next day and
we felt so sorry for him
that we let him back in
with her.

Then another very bad thing
happened.
Snip's friend Dotty , the
old, blind, deaf pony got
colic in the night and the
lady had to call the vet.

The vet was in Tipperary so the Lady had to walk Dotty up and down the driveway for two hours. Every time she stopped for a rest Dotty tried to lie down. Colic is like a very bad tummy ache and if you get it all you want to do is lie down but you can't because if you do you'll only get worse and die. By the time the vet arrived the Lady and Dotty were both exhausted.She gave Dotty some medicine and went away but it only helped for a little while and the Lady's face got very sad.

"She's gonna make Dotty sleep," said Frances.

"What that?" said MacDonald.

"It's when a pony gets very sick and the vet can't make it better so she gives it a little injection and it goes to sleep forever," said Pamela Anderson.

"It's dead then?"

"Yep"

"Does it hurt?"

"Nope."

We didn't want to see it so we went down to the willows at the bottom of the field. Only Pamela Anderson stayed with Dotty till the vet came back.

The vet's name was Gemma
and she was very kind and I
wrote her name in my
notebook in case I ever
needed to be made to sleep
I could ask for her.
After Dotty was asleep the
lady covered her with a rug
and told us we could come
and say goodbye if we
wanted to so we came and
grazed in the paddock
beside her for the night.
The lady was very upset but
not as upset as when the
little Ninja pony died. She
said Dotty was very old and
she'd had a good life since
she came to us and that's
what counted.

CHAPTER SIX-PAMELA ANDERSON GOES TO WEST CORK

A few days after Dotty went to sleep Florence fell ill. She couldnt get up and MacDonald stood over her for three days crying his little cob eyes out.

We thought she was going to die and Dog said she was going to eat her if she did. Dog was a horrible animal.

But Florence got better and got cheekier than ever, going wherever she liked and bringing Jemima and MacDonald with her. By then MacDonald had learned to speak sheep fluently and he hardly spoke pony any more at all.

Frances said leave him off, he's stupid enough to be a sheep anyway.

I hadn't made any more friends since the little Ninja Shetland died.

Sometimes the mouse stopped
for a chat but he was
always in a hurry to get to
wherever he was going. He
said his cat was proving
very difficult to train and
he might have to sell him
and buy another one.

Frances didn't seem to have
any friends either, she was
forever hiding in the
bushes up against the ditch
so one day I went to look
for her.
"Would you like to be my
friend?" I said.

I figured if I couldn't be
the Lady's favourite pony
the next best thing was to
be the favourite pony's
best friend.

At first Frances said she
didn't want to be my
friend, she didn't need
friends, but I kept going.

I followed her around and
showed her where the
juiciest grass was.

I even showed her my secret
hiding place in the top
paddock and still she
hardly spoke to me.

I'd almost given up when
one day she told me I was a
very handsome pony and she
liked me alot. After that
we went everywhere
together. We groomed each
other and grazed together
and the lady was so happy
to see us. I heard her tell
somebody that now she
couldn't rehome me even if
I got manners because what
would Frances do then, and
I wondered if it was
possible for the lady to
have two favourite ponies.
In spring three things
happened.

First Diablo discovered a small gap in the ditch and went into next door's. Next door's was fifteen acres with nothing on it, not even a cow. The lady had asked the old man who owned it if she could rent it but he wouldn't, we couldn't understand why, but Pamela Anderson, who knew everything, said that's Irish farmers for you, they'd rather leave it empty than do a bit of good by letting rescue ponies onto it.

So every night we went over the ditch and came back in the morning.

We were at it for six
months before the old man
spotted us and came around
to fight with the lady and
after that we couldn't go
any more but it didn't
really matter because we'd
had the whole summer and we
were as fat as fools by
then.
Not long after we started
going into next door's a
new pony came to live with
us.

He came from the pound in Cork and the Lady named him Boy George. He was a scoundrel. When Pamela Anderson called the Pony Council so he could tell us his story he said he was two years old and he was a member of the Mafia in Kilkenny and if we messed with him his friends would come and get us. We all burst out laughing.

"Would you listen to him?" said Diablo. "Mafia? And he not even come up to the Lady's kneecap."

Pamela Anderson gave Boy George her slitty eyed look.

"So how did you end up in
the pound, if you've so
many friends?" she said.
"We were on a robbery an
they left me behind when
the guards came. It was a
mistake. And they on their
way to bust me out the
pound only My Lovely Horse
Rescue took me out before
they got there."
"So why you here then? If
you belong to My Lovely
Horse Rescue, like?"
"I'm on a stopover on my
way to Dublin."
"Well, you don't look a day
over six months. Show me
your teeth," said Pamela
Anderson.

Boy George clamped his lips together and wouldn't let her see but later, when the Lady looked in his mouth she said Pamela Anderson was right, he was only six months old and should still be with his mammy. And worse than that. His mouth was cut at the corners. She said someone had been riding him and had put a piece of rope through his mouth.

Boy George soon became very sad and didn't want to eat because of his sore mouth and he ran away whenever he saw the Lady.

Sometimes that happens to ponies when they've never been loved. You'd think they'd be happy once they're saved and someone is nice to them but they're not used to it and it frightens them. It happened to me, too.

Frances been here three years and even though the lady loves her more than any other pony she's still frightened of her. She can't get used to being loved.

Boy George stayed for a month and he turned out to be a very sweet little pony in the end, once his mouth got better and he stopped telling stories about the Mafia.

By then we were very worried about MacDonald, how was he ever going to find his forever home? Who was going to adopt a pony who behaved like a sheep?

We'd almost given up on him when Florence, who was a terrible eavesdropper, told us the lady was planning to take three ponies to West Cork for summer grazing, she wouldn't have had to go at all if those evil sheep hadn't gobbled up all our grass.

Pamela Anderson held a Council meeting to decide who was going to go.

I was getting sick of meetings by then and I don't know why we had to have them because Pamela Anderson always got her own way never mind what anyone else said.

We decided that MacDonald should go to West Cork, maybe he'd have forgotten about Florence by the time he got back, and Pamela Anderson and Frances would go with him because nobody else wanted to go.

I wanted to go but Pamela Anderson said I was too naughty, and she wasn't chasing me all over West Cork when I broke out and ran away.
So off they went, Pamela Anderson, Frances and the wannabe sheep.

He wanted Florence to go with him but the lady said, no, absolutely not.

It was all going well until they got to the Bandon roundabout when Pamela Anderson opened the jockey door and nearly fell out onto the road. Luckily they were just pulling into the garage or the whole lot of them would have been loose on the motorway and Pamela Anderson was in trouble with the lady before she even arrived.

They were supposed to stay in West Cork for three months but it didn't work out that way.

They'd only been there
three weeks when Pamela
Anderson ate two trees and
destroyed the rockery.
After that MacDonald went
in the house and left muck
and grass all over the
place, fetlock deep it was.
Then Frances drank thirty
six bottles of Heineken and
left the empties in the
scullery and that was the
end of it. They got kicked
out and sent back here.
Frances said she didn't
care, the grass in West
Cork was rubbish anyway and
there were no trees and
bushes for her to hide
under.

"I was terrified for me life in case a dragon came out of the sky to eat me up," she said.

The lady should never have let her watch Game of Thrones, we all said so, but the lady's another one who thinks she knows everything so she didn't listen to us.

Now we had to put up with Frances yelling "Dragons!" every time she saw a crow or a seagull.

One day she barged right past me and knocked me flat trying to get to cover.

She'll forget about dragons
if she does it again and I
give her a clatter.

CHAPTER SEVEN-FLORENCE AND JEMIMA SAVE THE DAY

While they were away we'd
had a meeting with Dog
about the sheep.
"We should get rid of them
now, while the Lady's
away," said Diablo.

"And what you gonna tell
Macdonald when he gets back
and his mammy is gone?"
said Mario.

"I'll tell him they died,"
said Diablo.

"Oh that'll work," replied
Mario.

"Alright I'll tell him they
went to the factory to be
made into chops,"

"That bound to make him
feel better," said Mario.

"And anyway, how we gonna
get em to the factory? It's
miles away."

I soon got tired of
listening to them.

Pamela Anderson had put me in charge while she was away so I told them to shut up, no sheep going to the factory, forget it so they both kicked me but I told Pamela Anderson when she got back and she made them run around the track every day for two weeks so they didn't do it again.

The sheep laughed until their wool stood on end.

Being In Charge Pony was a big job and very hard work and most of the time nobody wanted to listen to me. I was very glad when Pamela Anderson came back and took over again. I was no good at that job. Sometimes you have to realise that you can't be good at everything and just try and be good at the things you are good at. Pamela Anderson was good at bossing everyone around and Mario was good at being the watchpony and Frances was good at mowing the lawn and telling lies. I knew I'd find out what I was good at one day if I kept on trying.

Luckily MacDonald had realised he wasn't a sheep while he was away in West Cork and went back to being a cob. so we started thinking about how to get rid of those pesky sheep again.

Pamela Anderson phoned the Department of Agriculture and told them the sheep had foot and mouth disease and they had an inspector over in half an hour, I wish they were that quick when people reported ponies starving in fields.

The inspector got very cross when he realised they didn't have foot and mouth and said he was going to report the lady for wasting taxpayer's money. He said they were in excellent condition.

"And why wouldn't they be? They been guzzling our grass all summer," said Diablo, but the inspector didn't speak pony so he didn't understand him. There was an awful hullabaloo when the lady got back from SuperValu and Pamela Anderson got her mobile confiscated again.

And then everything changed
when the sheep saved
Frances's life.
It happened like this. One
night MacDonald walked
through the fence in the
bottom paddock.

He was always walking
through fences, he didn't
care if the electric was on
or off, he just walked
through them, breaking the
lady's fence posts and
sending the wires flying
off in all directions.

The next day the lady went
to fix the fence and gather
up the wire but one piece
had landed in the long
grass and she didn't see it
and two nights later
Frances got caught in it.
It wrapped around her
fetlock and the more she
tried to get away the
tighter it became because
the other end was caught
around a tree stump.
Eventually she couldn't
move at all.We didn't know
what to do.
"Somebody's got to go and
call the lady," said Pamela
Anderson.

"How we gonna do that? Ever since HE arrived, the lady gone mad with the fencing," said Diablo. And he pointed at me.

We couldnt even make MacDonald break the fence again because he was serving two days in jail for the last time. We were desperate.

That's when Florence came to see what all the commotion was about.

"And you say sheep be stupid," she muttered.

She took Jemima and they got out under the fence and ran up to the house and stood outside the Lady's bedroom shouting.

Baa. Baaaaaaaa. Baaaaaaaaaaaaaaaaaaaaaaaaaaaaaa!

I'm sure they could hear them in Bonmahon, the racket they were making. The Lady got up and came out roaring.

"Do you know what time it is?"

The sheep said no, they
didn't know what time it
was but they'd find out but
in the meantime the lady
best follow them because
there was an emergency.
And bring pliers.

When Frances saw the Lady
coming she started twirling
and whirling, she wouldn't
stand still, I don't know
how the Lady managed to
clip that wire off the tree
stump but she did and as
soon as she was free
Frances ran off like the
mad eejit she is, with the
other end still tight
around her fetlock. The
Lady stood there with the
pliers in her hand, I could
see she didn't know what to
do but I knew where Frances
would be hiding because it
was our secret place so I
went to look for her.

"The lady says you've to come down to the garage where there's light so she can cut off the rest of that wire," I said, but Frances was too frightened to move.

"I'm not coming," she said and then she started to snap her teeth. When ponies snap their teeth it means they are very, very frightened. I'd never seen Frances do it before, nobody had.

I'm afraid of the
garage,too, I don't like
being in small spaces where
I can't run away but I knew
I had to be brave for
Frances
"What if I go with you?" I
said. So she followed me
but when we got to the
garage my nerve failed me
and I stopped.
I turned to look at
Frances.
"Will you go in?" I said
but she shook her head and
started snapping her teeth
again Something horrible
must have happened to her
in a garage.

I could see she was even
more afraid than me so I
took a deep breath and
opened my eyes as wide as I
could and stepped in and
Frances stepped in behind
me.

Frances told the lady she
was going to kick her head
off if she went anywhere
near her legs, she didn't
want to but she wouldn't be
able to stop herself
because she'd remember all
the horrible things that
had happened to her before.

The lady said, well
Frances, if you do that
I'll be dead and you'll
lose your leg so best you
try to forget about all the
horrible things that have
happened to you and behave
yourself.
Then she put on her hard
hat, just in case, and
knelt down by Frances's
hind leg. It took a long
time before she managed to
clip off the wire with the
red pliers because Frances
was so frightened. I was
frightened too but I stayed
with her the whole time.

The next day the lady said she was very proud of me. She said true courage is when you're frightened to do something but you do it anyway and she gave me a special award for bravery. It was a picture of the Little Ninja Shetland and I stuck it in my notebook. She didn't make me her favourite pony but somehow it didn't matter any more.

THE END

Made in the USA
Lexington, KY
25 March 2018